For Frania and Mina

With deep thanks to our agent, Angharad Kowal Stannus,
Mara Bergman and Nghiem Ta at Walker Books,
Stephan Hügel, Wendy Shakespeare, Marta Strass,
Coralie Bickford-Smith and Natalie Pangburn.

First published 2021 by Walker Books Ltd, 87 Vauxhall Walk, London SE11 5HJ

2 4 6 8 10 9 7 5 3 1

Text © 2021 Natalia O'Hara * Illustrations © 2021 Lauren O'Hara
Hand lettering by Natalia O'Hara

This book has been typeset in Joanna

Printed in China

British Library Cataloguing in Publication Data:
a catalogue record for this book is available from the British Library

ISBN 978-1-4063-8896-1 (Trade edition)

www.walker.co.uk

FRINDLESWYLDE

By

NATALIA and LAUREN O'HARA

WALKER BOOKS
AND SUBSIDIARIES

LONDON · BOSTON · SYDNEY · AUCKLAND

"Can you feel a tremble in the wind? The sun grows pale. The wild things hide.

"Frindleswylde is coming…

"Soon his face will peek from frozen ponds. The wild North wind will sing his name. He'll snatch the storks and hide the moon and pick the locks. As he creeps by, the bristling hills turn white as ghosts."

Granny shut the window and put another log on the fire.

"Poor storks!" said Cora, who was fond of a pair who lived on their roof. "But Frindleswylde would never snatch a child, would he, Granny?"

"Little one – old or young, kind or cruel, rich or poor, Frindleswylde snatches all. So promise to be wary when I'm out in the woods.

"Frindleswylde is cunning and he takes many shapes. If you open the door, he'll bring in the cold. If he brings in the cold, he'll put out the lamp. And if he puts out the lamp, I cannot come home to save you."

The lamp sat in a little round window in the attic. There it shone night and day, bright as a snowy owl's eye. When Granny finished work every night, she followed its golden light home through the woods.

"I promise!" said Cora. Then Granny lit her pipe and read fairy tales until supper, which was chicken soup with rolls shaped like crowns, and tiny golden pancakes with hot berries and cinnamon.

That same night, the first snow fell. Granny locked Cora's window and tucked her up tight. But all through the night, a silver birch in the yard knocked on the glass – *rap-tap-trap.*

"*Frindleswylde!*" Cora whispered. And she ran away to Granny's bed.

At dawn Granny went out to the yard to cut down the tree. But as she swung her axe it shook in her hand because inside the trunk was something as hard as a headstone. She whittled away the bark. Inside was a little child made out of ice. Granny dropped her axe in the snow.

The ice child looked exactly like Cora.

Granny hurried back to the house, but just then it began to snow. And by the time she reached the back door the ice child was already half buried. Its eyes – so like Cora's – looked fearful. So Granny turned back. She picked up the ice child, carried it into the kitchen and brushed the snow off its cheeks.

Then she picked up her tools and went to work. And as her steps died away, the ice child laughed.

Cora yawned, rubbed her eyes and screamed. Snow whistled down from the ceiling. Snow smothered the floor. Snow buried her quilt and bunny and pillow. "Granny!" she wailed. There was no reply, just a crash in the kitchen.

Cora crawled out of bed, snatched Granny's scarf to keep herself warm and tiptoed down the hall. In the living room, hailstones pounded the floor and cracked the windows. A blizzard howled in the bath. In the kitchen, a crow was nesting in the breadbin. And when she peered into Granny's pot she saw the dumplings in the soup had turned to snowballs. Cora heard footsteps above. "The lamp!" she cried, and scrabbled upstairs.

In the dim attic stood a boy as pale as a frosty morning. He had snow-white hair and eyes like the Arctic sea.

"Frindleswylde!" Cora whispered. "You're just a little boy."

"Oh, I am *everything*," said Frindleswylde. "And also nothing, which is far better!"

He plucked the lamplight with his fingers – it flickered like a caught butterfly – and dropped it into a hazelnut shell from the nut bowl. Then he snapped the shell shut, stepped back and fell out of the window.

Frindleswylde flipped through the air, bounced on his toes and tore through the gate laughing.

"Oh, what can I DO?" Cora cried. She couldn't chase Frindleswylde – she had never even left the yard alone. But without the lamp, Granny would be lost in the woods forever. And Cora would freeze alone in the frozen house.

Quick as a shiver, an icy wind roared up the stairs. It flew through the attic, took a sharp left and tossed Cora out of the window. She plunged downwards, her nightie flapping like a broken wing, and landed in a heap of snow. The wind pushed her across the yard, through the gate, into the woods and down to a fishpond.

Frindleswylde stood in a clump of spiky reeds, making little clouds with his fingers. When he saw Cora he smirked and leapt into the water. There was no sound or splash. That was strange, so Cora crept closer.

In the middle of the fishpond was a round, empty hole, like the one that dances over a plughole as the bath runs out. Gazing down, Cora thought about Granny, lost in the woods. Home, a wintery ruin. The lamplight, stolen and gone.

And down she leapt.

Down Cora fell, down and down. She flew past water and weeds and rocks.

And suddenly she landed in brightness and bitter cold.

She saw a meadow filled with a million flowers – lilies and delphiniums, bluebells, roses and glittering trilliums – shining as though every leaf had been dipped in sugar. Pink and white clouds drifted above, and looking closer Cora saw they were made of apple blossoms and cherry blossoms. Herons and hummingbirds hung still in the air, and in the distance a blue castle shivered on the pearly sky. It was too quiet, Cora thought. The only sound came from the flowers, which were so cold and stiff that as she passed they tinkled like the tiny bells on cat collars.

"Oh, hello!" whispered Cora. "How did you get here?" One of the storks from their roof stood alone in the grass. Cora reached out her hand. He was frozen stiff. She kissed his cold cheek and tied Granny's scarf around his neck.

"Ah-choo," said a lazy voice from behind.

Frindleswylde was lounging on an icy throne. "I *probably* caught cold in your mouldy old house," he said.

"There you are!" exclaimed Cora. "What is this place?"

"*This*," said Frindleswylde, "is where summer waits frozen for icy winter's end. This is the land that's ever ice. This is my home. And what are *you* doing here?"

"I've come to take our lamplight home," Cora said bravely, her voice trembling. "Please give it back, Frindleswylde! Or Granny will be lost in the woods forever."

Frindleswylde laughed. "Oh, who *cares?*" he said. "She's old. And silly. Anyway you're not *leaving*. I tricked you into coming and now you'll stay forever! I'll give you a dress of morning-frost and a polar bear and a garden full of statues. And if you aren't too annoying, I *might* make you Queen of Winter."

At this Cora started to cry.

"Stop that!" yelled Frindleswylde. "You're melting the grass." Which was true.

"Now *listen*," he said, "if you stop this ungodly leaking I shall make you a deal. I'll set three Impossible Tasks. If you complete them all, you can have your ugly yellow light and go if you want to. But if you don't, you shall stay here forever with me."

This sounded dreadful to Cora, but it was her only chance to save Granny. So she wiped her eyes on her nightie and nodded.

"Impossible Task One!" Frindleswylde sang, tugging off his boots. "I shall nap in my royal throne. Before I wake, you must turn hard to soft, and soft to hard." And with that he was snoring.

It truly is an Impossible Task! thought Cora. She felt like shaking Frindleswylde and stamping and howling and going to sleep all at once. But she remembered Granny lost in the woods, and sat down to think.

Perched on a stone, she saw a shimmery web of frost spreading across the floor from Frindleswylde's boots. When the frost met a little pool that Cora's tears had made, the tears froze. Cora had an idea. She took off her own boots and pulled on Frindleswylde's. They were cold as a mountain stream, but they fitted. She ran to the hole in the sky, wondering if there was a way back up. But there was not, and the hole was so far away that it looked like a peppercorn.

And then Cora felt cold feathers on the backs of her shins. "Hel–" she cried, but before she could say "p" or "me!" she was racing across the tingling sky, her face full of peach silk. "You unfroze!" she shouted, hugging the stork, and he clacked with pleasure. Past pink and white blossoms they soared, between frosty larks and up through the hole in the sky.

The stork shot up into Cora's world, and she dropped off his back. Down she hurtled, towards the deathly cold water of the fishpond. But instead of sinking, she slid. Cora looked down and saw ice curling out from Frindleswylde's boots like a net of stars. She laughed with delight. She twisted and leapt. Frost flew off her boots, giving the spiked reeds soft, feathery coats. And soon the pond was frozen solid.

That is how Cora turned hard reeds soft, and soft water icy hard.

Frindleswylde scowled as he tugged on his boots. Cora had crept back while he was snoring and dropped them by his throne. "Anyway," he grumbled, "that was a blubbery *baby* task for beginners. You'll be *addled* by this one!

"Impossible Task Two! I shall climb this cherry tree. Before I eat all the cherries, you must make the singing silent and the silent sing."

Frindleswylde leapt into the tree and began tossing frozen cherries into his mouth. But as he gobbled, his cloak pin fell to the ground. Cora saw it glittering in the grass and reached down. As she touched the frosty pin it brushed a pebble, which split like a sliced grape. Cora swished the pin back and forth, and made two tiny rips in the air. She smiled, placed it gently in her pocket and ran away to find the stork.

As they flew into her own world, Cora pointed to a village and the stork flapped down in the main square. There were bright houses, barns with tin roofs and a church with three bells that sang every hour. In the middle was a tall, icy fountain.

Trembling, Cora began to climb the fountain. When she reached the top she took the pin from her pocket, stretched up and pricked the bottom of a storm cloud. Hail poured down, battering her face. Cora screamed and tumbled into the pool below. Aching and wet, she longed to give up. But thinking of Granny lost in the woods, she climbed again.

This time Cora reached even higher, and jabbed the side of the cloud. Hail rushed out of the pinhole and the cloud shot away like a burst balloon. It hailed so hard that the roofs of the barns jangled and clattered. It hailed so hard the bells in the church fell out of the tower and rolled down the street.

That is how Cora made the singing bells silent and the silent roofs sing.

Under the fishpond, Frindleswylde was sticky and cherry-sick. "How did you do that?" he muttered, picking up his pin. "Well, my next task will be far more preposterous.

"Impossible Task Three!" he cried, dropping his coat on a frozen heron. "I shall take my bath in this icy stream. By the time my toes get wrinkly, you must turn black to white and white to black."

This task sounded even worse than the others. But as Frindleswylde warbled and splashed, Cora noticed snowflakes dropping from his coat onto the pebbles below. She threw on the coat, though it was cold as a blizzard, and scuttled away.

This time, when the stork flew into her world, Cora pointed at the sky. They rocketed upwards. It was bitterly cold and wind tore the treetops. "Slow down!" Cora shouted. But the stork couldn't hear. Cora slipped, hanging from his neck by her fingertips.

Then Frindleswylde's icy hood fell over her eyes, and she knew she would be able to hold on for only a second more. The cloak fanned out in the wind, and clouds and snow streamed off its hem. The clouds flew up to the sky. The snow fell down on the woods.

And thinking this wasn't the weather for jaunting, the stork turned home, catching Cora on his back as he plunged.

That is how Cora turned the white winter sky black with clouds, and the black woods white with snow.

"Oh, *fine*," said Frindleswylde when Cora returned. "You win." He threw her the nutshell.

"*That's* a funny kind of present!" said Cora, and she dropped it on the ground.

You see, when Cora wore Frindleswylde's boots her bones froze, and she could sense nothing.

When she wore his pin her heart froze, and she could feel nothing.

When she wore his coat her head froze, and she could remember nothing. Not the nutshell or the lamplight or her home in the woods.

So Frindleswylde gave Cora a crown instead. And a dress of morning frost and a polar bear and a garden full of statues. She thought these presents were much finer than a dusty old nutshell. She never guessed that Frindleswylde had tricked her. And when Cora wasn't looking, he stroked the stork's back and froze him solid.

And that is how Frindleswylde made Cora the Queen of Winter.

Together, they ruled every place where the North wind
sang. They raced polar bears across the tumbling sky, the Milky
Way crackling below. They dipped and plunged through the
Northern Lights and tripped out hooting, their skin stained
purple and bronze. They lay on their bellies in snow clouds,

watching porpoises leap the waves. And once, far below, they
heard the eerie song of mermaids. But sometimes Frindleswylde
cried, "Today we shall work!" And then they would freeze an
ocean or bury a city or hurl thunderbolts at a fleet of ships.

And the months flashed by like shooting stars.

One bright morning, the Queen of Winter was walking in her garden. Turning a corner she came across a statue she had never seen before. And though she could not sense with her bones or feel with her heart or remember with her head, her eyes saw Granny and they started to cry.

"What *are* you doing?" said a lazy voice from behind.

"Frindleswylde, you lied!" said the Queen. "You *said* I am Queen of Winter. You said I belong in this frozen place. But look – these drips fell out of my eyes and melted the grass. Inside me is warm!"

"Oh, it will go in the end," said Frindleswylde carelessly. "My warm did."

"Stop it!" yelled the Queen. She knew that whenever Frindleswylde didn't want to talk about anything, he talked about himself instead. "Tell me who I am."

Frindleswylde quickly pulled a hazelnut shell from around his neck and hid it behind his back. But the Queen saw him.

"I know that thing!" she said. "You gave it to me once, a long time ago. Let me see it – it's mine!"

"You are right" said Frindleswylde. He held out his hand. "But inside this nut is everything bad. If you take it you will grow and fade and *feel* things and end, like every one of these frozen ninnies. Please don't! Stay here with me. We'll play forever in this garden."

But she took the nutshell. And before Frindleswylde could take it back, she put it in her mouth and swallowed it.

The Queen felt light pouring over her tongue and down to her belly. It brought sounds and tastes and feelings – bites of hot apple cake, a woodpigeon singing close to the chimney, the flickering light of Friday night candles, an armful of lilacs in summer rain…

Cora remembered home. Her bones and her heart and her head grew warm. She looked up, rubbing her eyes.

"Granny!" she screamed. She ran across the grass and flung her arms around the statue. She rubbed its stiff hands and tried to button its coat.

But the statue was hard, silent and white.

Cora walked away sobbing. *Granny is frozen*, she thought. *She's gone.*

But *then*, Cora thought, *so was I*. She thought about the secrets in things – like winter in a young tree, light in a nutshell or warmth in a frozen child waiting to spring out. Everything changes, then changes again.

Cora ran back and kissed the statue's hard cheek. "Granny," she said, "I've been thinking. There's nothing to be scared of."

And whether it was Cora's warm breath or the words she said, Granny stirred. She blinked and smiled. "Hello, little pea," she said, and hugged her tight.

"Granny, let's go home," said Cora. She led the way to the hole in the sky. And she was so full of lamplight that wherever she went, flowers shook their petals and birds sang.

But what about Frindleswylde? He was hiding behind his throne, watching Cora. And when he saw her walking away with Granny he flew into a rage. "If she won't be a queen in my palace," he cried, "she will be a statue in my garden!"

Beneath the hole in the sky, the stork and his mate were awake and clattering. They carried Cora and Granny up through the fishpond and into the world. After them flew birds, dragonflies, bees and butterflies. Blossom clouds swooped through the air like white dragons, perching on bare branches.

But Frindleswylde was not far behind. He rose out of the

pond in a freezing fog, snowflakes swirling about him like soldiers around their fort.

Just then a tiny golden butterfly landed on Frindleswylde's nose. He sneezed and waved off the fog. He looked round in disgust. *Spring* had come! Shivering, Frindleswylde leapt back down the hole in the pond. And there he stayed, slumbering on a heap of ice until winter.

Cora and Granny strolled home through the sunlit woods.
When they got back, Granny fixed the broken windows and
threw out the crows. Cora picked up the attic lamp, and she
was still so full of light that it lit by itself.

And that night, instead of asking for a story, Cora told one.
She told how she had leapt into a world of silence and ice,
completed three Impossible Tasks, been tricked and become
the Queen of Winter. She told how she had outsmarted
Frindleswylde, found warmth inside and brought spring to
their woods. Cora talked until the moon peeped in at the
window and Granny's eyes were as round as two stars.

After that, life mostly went back to how it was before.
There was apple picking and fairy tales and hot berry pancakes.
But now while Granny worked, Cora drew maps in the woods
or read to the storks or played with her friends. And she shot
up like a young pea plant.

Soon it was winter again. One frosty night, Granny saw that Cora's window was open just a crack. She asked why, and Cora said it was in case Frindleswylde came to visit.

"But, Cora!" cried Granny. "Aren't you scared?"

"Oh no," said Cora. "That little goose sleeps on ice all summer. I'm bigger than him now."

Years passed, but Frindleswylde never came. Cora thought he had forgotten her long ago, and perhaps that was true. But every year on the night the first snow fell, a tiny frost crown appeared on her windowpane. Cora never knew, though. Because when the first rays of light peeked through the woods, it was gone.